Dear Parents:

Congratulations! Your child is taking the first steps on an exciting journey. The destination? Independent reading!

STEP INTO READING® will help your child get there. The program offers five steps to reading success. Each step includes fun stories and colorful art or photographs. In addition to original fiction and books with favorite characters, there are Step into Reading Non-Fiction Readers, Phonics Readers and Boxed Sets, Sticker Readers, and Comic Readers—a complete literacy program with something to interest every child.

Learning to Read, Step by Step!

Ready to Read   Preschool–Kindergarten
• big type and easy words • rhyme and rhythm • picture clues
For children who know the alphabet and are eager to begin reading.

Reading with Help   Preschool–Grade 1
• basic vocabulary • short sentences • simple stories
For children who recognize familiar words and sound out new words with help.

Reading on Your Own   Grades 1–3
• engaging characters • easy-to-follow plots • popular topics
For children who are ready to read on their own.

Reading Paragraphs   Grades 2–3
• challenging vocabulary • short paragraphs • exciting stories
For newly independent readers who read simple sentences with confidence.

Ready for Chapters   Grades 2–4
• chapters • longer paragraphs • full-color art
For children who want to take the plunge into chapter books but still like colorful pictures.

STEP INTO READING® is designed to give every child a successful reading experience. The grade levels are only guides; children will progress through the steps at their own speed, developing confidence in their reading.

Remember, a lifetime love of reading starts with a single step!

Published in the United States by Random House Children's Books, a division of Penguin Random House LLC, 1745 Broadway, New York, NY 10019, and in Canada by Penguin Random House Canada Limited, Toronto.

Step into Reading, Random House, and the Random House colophon are registered trademarks of Penguin Random House LLC.

Visit us on the Web!
StepIntoReading.com
rhcbooks.com

Educators and librarians, for a variety of teaching tools, visit us at RHTeachersLibrarians.com

ISBN 978-0-593-12802-2 (trade)
ISBN 978-0-593-12803-9 (lib. bdg.)
ISBN 978-0-593-12804-6 (ebook)

Printed in the United States of America   10 9 8 7 6 5 4 3 2 1

BATMAN™

HARLEY AT BAT!

by Arie Kaplan

illustrated by Fabio Laguna, Marco Lesko,
and Beverly Johnson

Batman created by Bob Kane with Bill Finger

Random House 🏠 New York

Inside a Gotham City jewelry
store, a pair of thieves
held a rare white diamond.
It was as big as a baseball!
Batman was about
to swoop down on
the thieves,
when suddenly—

KA-BOOM!
The wall exploded,
and the villain Harley Quinn
roared in on her motorcycle!

Harley snatched the diamond
from the shocked thieves.

"Ooh, it's sparkly," she said.

Harley laughed
as she spun around
and left through
the hole in the wall.

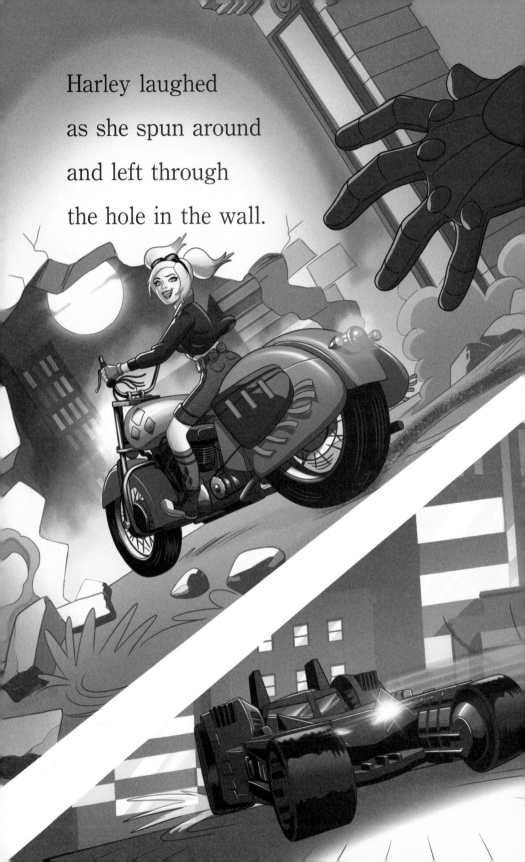

Batman leaped into the Batmobile and chased her!

Batman sped past Harley.
He turned the Batmobile
right in front of her,
blocking her path.

10

Harley tossed colorful water balloons
at the Batmobile.

She laughed and revved her engine.

The balloons were glitter bombs!
SPLOOSH! SPLOOSH! SPLOOSH!
The Batmobile's windshield
was covered with glittery paint.

Batman couldn't see Harley

as she rode off into the night.

Batman decided to follow
Harley on foot.
A trail of glitter led him
to Gotham City Stadium.

Batman noticed lights
coming from the stadium.
"It's too late for a
baseball game,"
he said.

When Batman reached the stadium,
he couldn't believe what he saw.
Harley had joined the Joker
and his henchmen on the field.

They were all playing baseball—
using the priceless diamond
as the ball!

"Stop right there!" Batman said.

"Sorry!" Harley cried.

"Even you can't stop
   the Prankster Playoffs."

"The what?" Batman asked.

"Every year," Harley explained, "the Joker and I play a ballgame with a different rare gem— DUCK!"

The Joker pitched the diamond.

It roared toward home plate.

Batman ducked just in time
as Harley swung her mallet.

THOCK!

Harley hit the diamond
high in the air!
She pushed past Batman
and started running!

The Joker and his goons cheered
as the diamond sailed
into the outfield.

This was Batman's chance!
He used gas to knock out
two of the Joker's goons.

At the same time,

Harley rounded first base.

She did a cartwheel before moving on!

Harley stayed focused on the game.

When she passed second base,

she didn't notice Batman

lassoing the third goon.

Batman looked for the Joker.

The villain had found the gem!

The criminal clown cackled,

"Now, that's what I call

a baseball diamond!"

While Harley rounded third base,
Batman grabbed the Joker.

The hero had caught him off-base!

He quickly tied the villain up.

"Foul ball," the Joker grumbled.

As Harley slid into home plate,
the umpire yelled, "You're OUT!"
Harley shouted, "I'm safe!"

The umpire removed his mask

and held up a pair of Bat-Cuffs.

It was Batman!

Moments later, all the criminals
were tied up on the pitcher's mound.
"It was my turn at bat," Harley pouted,
"until Batman called me out!"